DATE DUE

SAINT PATRICK

by Ann Tompert
Illustrated by Michael Garland

Boyds Mills Press

For Katheryn, who started the ball rolling
—A. T.

For the nuns and priests of my youth
—M. G.

Text copyright © 1998 by Ann Tompert
Illustrations © 1998 by Michael Garland

Published by Caroline House
Boyds Mills Press, Inc.
A Highlights Company
815 Church Street
Honesdale, Pennsylvania 18431
Printed in China

Publisher Cataloging-in-Publication Data
Tompert, Ann.
    Saint Patrick / by Ann Tompert ; illustrated by Michael Garland.—1st ed.
[32]p. : col.ill. ; cm.
Summary : A picture book biography of the patron saint of Ireland.
ISBN 1-56397-659-5
1. Patrick, Saint, 373?-463?—Biography—Juvenile literature. 2. Christian saints—
Ireland—Juvenile literature. [1. Patrick, Saint, 373?-463?—Biography. 2. Christian
saints—Ireland.]
I. Garland, Michael, ill. II. Title.
    [B]—dc21   1998   AC   CIP
Library of Congress Catalog Card Number 97-72774

First edition, 1998
Book designed by Tim Gillner and Michael Garland
The text of this book is set in 14-point Usherwood Medium.
The illustrations are done in mixed media.

10 9 8 7 6 5 4

I arise today
Through the strength of heaven:
Light of sun,
Radiance of moon,
Splendor of fire,
Speed of lightning,
Swiftness of wind,
Depth of sea,
Stability of earth,
Firmness of rock.

—Saint Patrick

Long ago in the fourth century, a boy was born in southwest Britain near the Irish Sea. His name was Succat. But later in his life, he was known as Patrick.

Patrick's father, Calpurnicus, was a well-to-do landowner and a member of the town council. He was also a deacon in the Church. However, Patrick was not a religious boy.

"I did not know the true God," he said. "I did not keep His commandments."

Patrick grew up in a comfortable home. He
had good food to eat. He had fine clothes to wear.
He went to school, but he was a poor student.
Although his father knew Latin, the language of
learning, Patrick did not speak or write it very
well.

"I did not study like the others," he said.

When Patrick was about sixteen, Irish pirates swept down upon the coast of Britain, blowing their bronze war trumpets. They looted villages and killed those who resisted. Patrick, along with many other Britons, was captured and shipped across the Irish Sea, where he was sold into slavery.

Patrick was sold to one of Ireland's many chieftains, who were called kings. He was taken to northwest Ireland near the Western Sea, the ancient name of the Atlantic Ocean.

There he was put to work tending his master's sheep and cattle. The work was hard. The winds whipped him about. The rains soaked him to the skin, and frost froze him to the bone. But he was not treated harshly by his master.

"I was saved from all evil," he said.

While Patrick was alone with his master's sheep and cattle, he had time to think. He remembered the good times he had had at home. He remembered how he had paid little attention to the teachings of the Church. He fasted and prayed.

"The love of God came to me more and more," he said. "I would say a hundred prayers during the day and almost as many in the night."

Patrick had been a slave for almost six years when one night he heard a voice in his sleep.

"You will soon go to your own country," the voice said.

A few nights later, he heard the voice again.

"Your ship is ready," it said.

To find his ship, Patrick knew he would have to travel to the Irish Sea, two hundred miles away. Yet he set out one night to find the ship and freedom.

"I had never been there," he said. "I knew no one."

Patrick was sure his master would send a search party to capture him, so he traveled during the night and hid by day. He trudged over mountainous land. He worked his way through forests where brambles slashed his arms and legs and ripped his clothes. He slogged through bogs where the mud gripped his feet, trying to hold him prisoner.

He often went hungry, eating only roots and berries. Although he suffered many hardships, Patrick never lost hope.

"God kept directing my path," he said. "I feared nothing."

At last he came to a port on the Irish Sea. There he found a boat preparing to sail. He asked if he might go along. His request angered the captain.

"You cannot travel with us," the captain shouted.

Patrick turned away, and as he walked, he prayed that the captain would change his mind. Before he finished praying, the captain called him back, and they set sail at once.

After sailing for three days, they landed on the shores of Britain. The land was covered with thick forests. For almost a month, Patrick and the other men wandered in the woods. The captain feared they would never find their way out. The men suffered from hunger.

"Many had collapsed," Patrick said.

The captain, a pagan, asked Patrick for help.

"Tell me, Christian," he said. "You say that your God is great and all-powerful. Why, then, do you not pray for us?"

"Turn in faith to the Lord, my God," said Patrick. "Ask *Him* to send food."

The captain and his men followed Patrick's advice. And that same day, a herd of pigs appeared.

"From that day onward," said Patrick, "we had abundant food."

After resting for two days, they traveled for several more before they came at last to a village.

Patrick left the men and continued his journey. When he finally reached home, his parents embraced him.

"After all the troubles I experienced," Patrick said, "they earnestly requested that I never leave them again."

Patrick was content to stay at home until he had a dream that changed his life.

"I saw in my dream a man who had countless letters from the people of Ireland," he said. "They asked me to come back and walk among them once more."

Because of this dream, Patrick believed that he was chosen by God to convert the people of Ireland to Christianity. His family and friends tried to persuade him to stay home. But Patrick knew what he had to do with his life.

"I live for God," he told them, "and to teach the Irish heathens."

Setting aside family, luxury, and comfort, he sailed across the English Channel to Gaul, which we now call France. He spent several years preparing for his mission. He studied to become a deacon and later was ordained a priest.

In time he was made a bishop. It was then that he set out with a group of followers to brave the dangers of barbarous Ireland. Even after years of study, Patrick felt he was not well prepared for his mission. He knew, however, that God would protect him and guide him.

Patrick baptized and confirmed thousands of Irish people. He ordained priests. He helped those who wanted to become monks and nuns. He traveled throughout Ireland preaching to all who would listen.

"I went everywhere," he said, "even to the farthest districts, beyond which nobody had ever gone."

And always, Patrick faced many dangers from people who did not want to change their pagan ways. He was threatened. He was imprisoned. And again, he was enslaved.

Patrick recounted how his enemies seized him and his companions.

"They wished to kill me. They took away everything they found, and they put me in irons. On the fourteenth day, the Lord delivered me from their power and our belongings were returned to us."

Patrick stayed in Ireland for more than thirty years. Besides facing persecution by Irish pagans, he battled the pangs of homesickness.

"How I wanted to go to Britain, to my fatherland and my parents," he said.

His wish was not to be. On March 17, in about the year 461, Patrick died.

But his work lived on. He became known as the apostle to Ireland and its patron saint. All Ireland became Christian because the priests, monks, and nuns he left behind continued to spread Patrick's message, inspirited by his words:

"We ought to fish well and diligently as the Lord teaches, saying, 'I will make you fishers of men.' We should spread our nets to take a great throng for God. Everywhere there should be clergy to baptize and exhort the poverty-stricken and needy folk."

AUTHOR'S NOTE

One of the earliest known biographies of St. Patrick was written by Muirchu in the seventh century. By then, memories of Patrick were vague and confused. But he is generally believed to have been born in Roman Britain around the year 385.

Through the centuries, many more biographies have been written. They often contain legends that have grown about St. Patrick, including two that are especially well known.

One legend tells how St. Patrick used a shamrock to explain the Holy Trinity. Shamrocks are small, clover-like green plants with three leaves. When a group of people he was preaching to found it difficult to understand how three persons could be in one God, St. Patrick picked a shamrock that was growing at his feet. He showed it to them.

"Is it any more unusual that three persons should be united in one God than it is for three leaves of the shamrock to grow on one stem?" he asked.

Many people wear a shamrock on St. Patrick's Day in remembrance of this legend.

The other well-known legend recounts how St. Patrick rid Ireland of snakes by driving them into the Irish Sea. One stubborn serpent refused to go. St. Patrick invited him into a box he had made. But the snake refused to enter it.

"It's too small," he said.

"I don't think so," said St. Patrick.

"Yes, it is," said the snake.

They argued about it for some time until at last the serpent said, "I'll prove it's too small."

With that he climbed into the box. St. Patrick slammed down the lid and threw the box into the sea.

The only authentic sources of knowledge about St. Patrick's life are two letters he wrote. One is "Confession," written in his old age when his long career was almost over. The other is "Letter to the Soldiers of Coroticus."

In this biography, I used "Confession" as the main source of information. I also relied upon the interpretations suggested by various authors who have studied the "Confession," using those that seemed most logical to me.